Hop Up! Wriggle

Over!

BY Elizabeth Honey

CLARION BOOKS ⊚ Houghton Mifflin Harcourt ⊚ Boston New York

Wakey wakey

Hungry

Crunch crunch

Gobble gobble

Come on, slowpoke!

Hop up! Wriggle over! Whoo!

Peas for supper

Easy peasy!

Chomp chomp
Munch munch!

Brush your . . .   pearly whites!

Hop up! Wriggle over! Pipe down!

Ready?

Curl up

Snuggle down

Sweet dreams...

Ahhhh!

Zzzzz...

ELIZABETH HONEY is an award-winning author of poetry, picture books, and novels who lives in Melbourne, Australia. She knows the animals in this book by the following names:

 quoll (kwall)

 wallaby (WALL-ah-bee)

echidna (i-KID-nah)

possum (POSS-uhm)

 wombat (WAHM-bat)

antechinus (an-teh-KIGH-ness)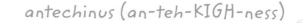

Can you find all nine of Koala and Kangaroo's
baby animals in each scene in this book?

koala (koh-WAH-lah)

kangaroo (kan-geh-ROO)

numbat (NUM-bat)

bilby (BILL-bee)

quokka (KWA-kah)

Elizabeth dedicates this book to Wendy and Alan Reid,
for teaching us to notice what's happening in nature.

Clarion Books, 3 Park Avenue, New York, New York 10016 • Copyright © 2015 by Elizabeth Honey • First published in Australia in 2015 by Allen & Unwin • First U.S. edition 2017

All rights reserved. Clarion Books is an imprint of Houghton Mifflin Harcourt Publishing Company. • www.hmhco.com

Library of Congress Cataloging-in-Publication Data is available. • ISBN 978-0-544-79084-1 • Manufactured in China • SCP 10 9 8 7 6 5 4 3 2 1 • 4500640599